THE TROPIC *of* SERPENTS

A MEMOIR BY LADY TRENT

MARIE BRENNAN

TITAN BOOKS

The Tropic of Serpents
Print edition ISBN: 9781783292417
E-book ISBN: 9781783292424

Published by Titan Books
A division of Titan Publishing Group Ltd
144 Southwark Street, London SE1 0UP

First edition: June 2014
10 9 8 7 6 5

A CIP catalogue record for this title is available from the British Library.

Printed and bound in the UK by CPI Group Ltd.

What did you think of this book? We love to hear from our readers. Please email us at: readerfeedback@titanemail.com, or write to us at the above address.

To receive advance information, news, competitions, and exclusive offers online, please sign up for the Titan newsletter on our website.

WWW.TITANBOOKS.COM